RABBIT and HEDGEHOG

TREASURY

ANDERSEN PRESS

THE BIRTHDAY PRESENTS

Rabbit and Hedgehog don't know when each other's birthdays are, so they decide to celebrate tomorrow, just in case.

"Hedgehog," said Rabbit. "When is your birthday?"
"I don't know," said Hedgehog.
Rabbit sighed. "Neither do I," he said.

"If I don't know when my birthday is,"
said Hedgehog, "how could you?"
"I mean," said Rabbit, "I don't know
when *my* birthday is."
"Ah," said Hedgehog.

As the sun sank behind the trees,
Hedgehog and Rabbit thought sadly of
all the birthdays they would never have.

"I have an idea," said Hedgehog.

"Let's celebrate our birthdays tomorrow."

"But they might not be tomorrow," said Rabbit.

"But they *might* be," said Hedgehog.

"It will be a shame to miss them if they are."

"You are right," said Rabbit. "It is a good idea.
We will wish each other Happy Birthday."
"We will give each other presents," said Hedgehog.
"Presents?" yawned Rabbit.
"Birthday presents," said Hedgehog. "That's what
birthdays are for."

Later, as Hedgehog snuffled for slugs
beneath the plump, silver moon,
he wondered what present to give his friend.

Hedgehog thought about under-the-earth
where Rabbit was fast asleep.
"How silent and gloomy and damp it must be.
How dark!"

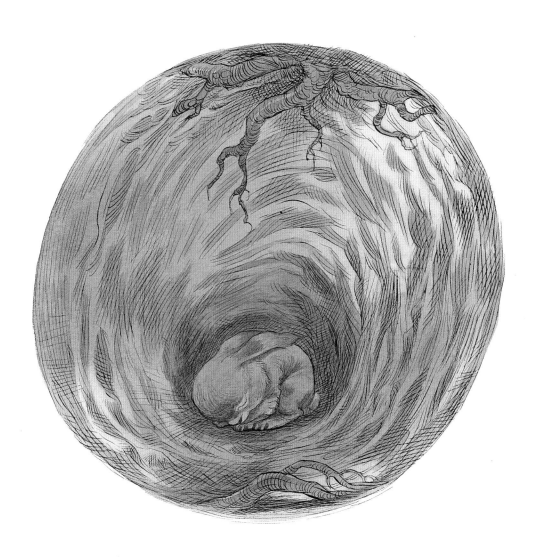

An empty bottle glinted down by the lake.
Hedgehog looked at the bottle.
Hedgehog looked at the moon on the water.
"That's it!" he cried.

Hedgehog filled the bottle with the bright water.

"A bottle of moonlight shall be my present," he said.
Then he wrapped it up and went to bed.

Rabbit woke early, too excited to stay asleep.
"What present should I give to Hedgehog?"
he wondered.

Rabbit thought of his friend,
sleeping in the wide open up-there.
"How frightening and noisy it must be.
How bright!"

In the corner of his burrow,
he spied his useful tin.
"The very thing!" he cried.

Rabbit filled the tin with warm,
snuggly darkness and patted
it down with his paw.
"A box of cosiness," he said.

He pressed the lid into place

and wrapped it all up with straw.
"Hedgehog will love my present."

Evening came. The two friends met.

"Rabbit," said Hedgehog. "Happy Birthday!"

"Hedgehog," said Rabbit. "Happy Birthday to you!"

"Here is a present for you," said Hedgehog.
Rabbit tore off the wrapping-leaf.
"It's a bottle of moonlight," said Hedgehog,
"so that you will no longer be afraid of the
very-very dark in your burrow."

"But I'm not..."
Rabbit stopped.
"Thank you," he said. "It's a wonderful present."

"And here is *your* present," said Rabbit.
Hedgehog tore off the wrapping-straw.

"It's a box of cosiness," said Rabbit,
"so that you will no longer be
disturbed by the bright, noisy day."

"But I'm not..."
Hedgehog stopped.
"It's just what I've always wanted," he said.

In the middle of the dark night,
Rabbit woke and looked at his present.
"Dear Hedgehog," he said.
"A bottle of moonlight, indeed."
He took out the stopper
and drank the water inside.
"I can fill it with water every day," said Rabbit.
"Then I will never be thirsty in the night again."

At the end of the long, rustling night,
Hedgehog noticed his present.
"Dear Rabbit," he said, sleepily.
"A box of cosiness, indeed!"
Hedghog opened the lid and looked inside.
"It's a slug-catcher!" he said.
"I will never be hungry if I wake up in the day again."

That evening, Hedgehog found Rabbit
down by the lake.
"Do you like your bottle of light?" he said.

"Yes," said Rabbit. "It's the best present
I've ever had. Do you like your box of cosiness?"
"Yes," said Hedgehog. "It's the best present
I've ever had."

Together, the two friends watched the sun
turn from orange to red.

"Hedgehog," said Rabbit, rubbing his eyes.
"When shall we have another birthday?"
"Soon," said Hedgehog. "Very soon."

RABBIT'S WISH

Rabbit wants more than anything for Hedgehog to stay awake all day with him. Will his wish come true?

"Look at the sky, Hedgehog," said Rabbit. "It's all beautiful and red."

"I like it better when it's twinkly and black," said Hedgehog. "Besides, you know what they say about red skies."

"Remind me," said Rabbit.

"Red sky in the morning, shepherd's warning," said Hedgehog. "Rain is on its way."

Hedgehog yawned. "Time for me to go to bed," he said.

"So soon?" said Rabbit.

"Yes, Rabbit," said Hedgehog. "You are a day creature and I am a night creature. That is the way it is."

Rabbit nodded sadly.

"Night-night, Hedgehog. I mean, *day-day*!"

As Hedgehog disappeared from view, Rabbit sighed a great big, lonely sigh. "I wish," he said, "that just for once, Hedgehog could stay up all day with me."

With his friend gone, Rabbit did what he always did.
He had breakfast.

A little grass...

A dandelion leaf...

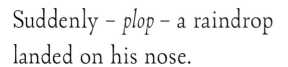

Suddenly – *plop* – a raindrop
landed on his nose.

"Bother!" said Rabbit. "Hedgehog was right. Rain was on its way. And now it's here!"

As Rabbit hopped back to his burrow, the rain grew heavier and heavier. "How wet it is!" he said.

Rabbit shook the water from his fur, wiped the mud from
his paws, and scampered underground.

"My burrow," said Rabbit happily. "So warm. So cosy.
So *dry*!" He frowned. "But it is also rather messy,"
he said. "As it is raining *out*side, I will stay *in*side
and tidy up."

Rabbit busied himself all morning.

He swept the floor.

He made his bed.

He sorted through his treasures, one by one...

The ball.　　　The string.　　　The woolly thing.

And most precious of all, the bottle of moonlight that Hedgehog had given him. "Oh, Hedgehog, I *do* miss you," said Rabbit. "I…"

"Water!" Rabbit cried. "There's water in my burrow!"
The water was trickling down the tunnel and seeping up
through the floor. It quickly soaked Rabbit's bed of straw,
and set his treasures bobbing.

With the bottle of moonlight in one arm, and the ball, the
string and the woolly thing in the other, Rabbit hurried
from his burrow.

Rabbit couldn't believe his eyes.
The rain was heavier than ever.
And the lake! It was higher than he had seen it
before – so high that Rabbit's little hill had been
turned into an island.

Far away, on the other side of the lake, the tops of
Hedgehog's bramble patch poked up above the
swirling, muddy water.
Rabbit dropped his treasures. He ran this way and that.
"Hedgehog!" he cried. "Hedgehog, where are you?"

"Here I am," said a little voice.
Rabbit spun round. Hedgehog was standing
down by the water's edge.

"Hedgehog!" cried Rabbit.

"Rabbit!" cried Hedgehog.

"I was so *worried!*" said Rabbit.

"There was no need to be worried," said Hedgehog.

"I'm a good swimmer. When the water woke me, I was worried about *you!* So I swam across the lake to find you."

Rabbit stared at his friend with wide-open eyes.
"You're so brave!" he said. "But you mustn't catch cold."
He put the woolly thing on Hedgehog's head.

"But what are we going to do *now*, Hedgehog?" said Rabbit. "My burrow is full of water. Your bed is at the bottom of the lake. And it's *still* raining!"

"I know just what we can do," said Hedgehog. "We can play."

"Yes!" said Rabbit. "We can play together in the rain."

They played catch.

They played tug-of-war.

They played boats.

The rain stopped, the sky cleared and the stars came out.
Rabbit and Hedgehog sat down at the edge of the lake.
"Hedgehog," said Rabbit. "I have a confession."
"What do you mean?" said Hedgehog.
"I have something to tell you," said Rabbit...

"It was my fault that everything happened.
I wished that you could stay up all day with me."
He looked down sorrowfully. "And my wish came true."
"I'm glad that it did," said Hedgehog. "Maybe next time
I will wish that you could stay up all night. With me!"
"I'd like that," said Rabbit. He yawned.
"But now it's time for me to go to bed."

"Night-night, Rabbit," said Hedgehog.
"Night-night, Hedgehog," said Rabbit.

WHAT DO YOU REMEMBER?

*Hedgehog wants to play a remembering game,
but Rabbit thinks they will end up
arguing, just like last time.*

"Rabbit," said Hedgehog. "Let's play 'Remembering'."
"I don't want to," said Rabbit. "You know what always happens."
"*Please*, Rabbit," said Hedgehog. "It won't happen this time. I promise."
"Oh, all right," said Rabbit. "If you promise."

"Close your eyes," said Hedgehog.
Rabbit closed his eyes.
Hedgehog led him away.

"Where do you think we are?" said Hedgehog.
Rabbit twitched his nose. The air smelled damp
and leafy. "I think we're in the wood," he said.

"Open your eyes!" said Hedgehog.
Rabbit opened his eyes. They *were* in the wood.

"June, July, September,
what do you remember?"
said Hedgehog.
"I... I remember..."
Rabbit began.

"You climbed on to
the tree-stump," said
Hedgehog excitedly.
"You wobbled about.
Like this."
"No," said Rabbit,
a little hurt.
"I was *dancing.*"

"Then you fell off," said Hedgehog.

"I *jumped*," said Rabbit.

"My turn," said Hedgehog. He closed his eyes.
Rabbit led him out of the woods.

At the top of the ridge, he stopped and placed
an acorn in Hedgehog's paw.
"Open your eyes," he said.
"Say the rhyme," said Hedgehog.
"June, July, September, what do you remember?"
said Rabbit.

"We each had an acorn," said Hedgehog, "just like this one. We had an acorn-rolling competition." He turned to Rabbit. "You kept dropping yours."

"I was bouncing it," said Rabbit very quietly.
"Rabbit," said Hedgehog, "that was too easy.
I want another go."

Hedgehog closed his eyes again. Rabbit took him
down to the stepping-stones.

"Well?" said Rabbit.
"You've forgotten the rhyme again," said Hedgehog.
"June, July, September," said Rabbit rather impatiently.
"What do you remember?"

Hedgehog jumped on to the
first stepping-stone.
"I remember a hot,
dry day," he said.
"The stream was low.
We crossed to the island –
and you nearly fell in."

"I didn't!" said Rabbit.
"You tripped," said Hedgehog.
"I caught you."
"I was picking up a water-snail,"
said Rabbit. "For *you*."

"I don't remember
a water-snail,"
said Hedgehog.

"I dropped it,"
said Rabbit.
"When you
grabbed me."

67

Hedgehog jumped to the second stepping-stone.
"No, no, Rabbit," he said.
"You've got it all wrong again."

"Oh, Hedgehog!" said Rabbit crossly.
"This is what always happens when
we play 'Remembering'.
And you promised it wouldn't!
You get all bossy and showy-offy.
You tell me my memories
are wrong."

"But they *are* wrong,"
said Hedgehog.
"You did trip.
I did catch you."

"*Hmmph!*"
said Rabbit.

Rabbit turned his back on Hedgehog.
He sat on the ground.
He folded his arms.
"It's not *my* fault that you're so full of forget," said Hedgehog.

"I'm not listening," said Rabbit.
He put his paws over his ears.
"*Hm, hm, hm, hm,*"
he hummed.

"I REMEMBER *EVERYTHING!*"
Hedgehog shouted.
He turned and jumped to the third stepping-stone, and...

SPLASH!

Rabbit jumped up. "Oh, Hedgehog!" he said, as he hurried to help him. "You forgot that the third stepping-stone wobbles."

"You're right," said Hedgehog. "So I didn't remember *everything* after all."

"I'm sorry I got cross," said Rabbit.

"I'm sorry I made you cross," said Hedgehog.

"Well, I'm sorry I made you make me cross," said Rabbit.

"Rabbit," said Hedgehog. "Can we be friends again?"
"Of course we can, Hedgehog!" said Rabbit.
"*Best* friends."

"Hedgehog," said Rabbit. "There is something I really don't remember. I don't remember the first time we met. Do you?"

Hedgehog thought. And thought and thought.

He sucked his paw and scratched his head.

"No, Rabbit," he said at last. "That is something I don't remember. I feel as if I've known you for ever."

Rabbit nodded. "That's just how I feel, Hedgehog," he said. "For ever and ever."

A LITTLE BIT OF WINTER

It's time for Hedgehog to hibernate,
but he's sad that he will never see winter.
Can Rabbit find a way to show him?

"I'll miss you," said Rabbit. "Will you miss me?"

"No," said Hedgehog.

"I'll miss *you*," said Rabbit.

"I know," said Hedgehog, "you have just told me."

"You are forgetful," said Hedgehog.

"Forgetful?" said Rabbit.

"If you were not," said Hedgehog, "you would remember *why* I will not miss you."

"Remind me," said Rabbit.

"I will be asleep," said Hedgehog. "You do not miss friends when you are asleep."

Hedgehog picked up a little, sharp stone
and walked to the tree.
Rabbit ate a little green grass, and then
a dandelion leaf, and then some clover.
Hedgehog wrote a message on the bark.

"Rabbit," said Hedgehog, "there is something I want you to do for me. It will be hard for an animal who is so full of forget. So I have written a message – to remind you. I want you to save me a little bit of winter."

"But why?" said Rabbit.

"I want to know what winter *feels* like," said Hedgehog.

"Winter is hard and white," said Rabbit.

"Winter is cold."

"But what *is* cold?"
said Hedgehog.

"I am cold now.
Cold and...
sle-e-e-e-py."
He yawned.

Rabbit prodded his friend. "Ouch," he cried.

"Rabbit," said Hedgehog. "It is time for me to find somewhere warm to spend the winter."

Rabbit sucked his paw. "I'll miss you," he said.

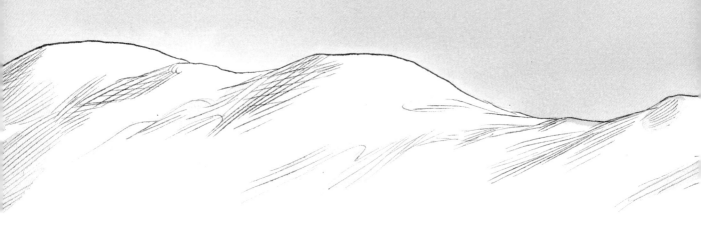

Winter was bad that year. Snow fell. The lake
turned to ice. Rabbit was warm in his burrow,
but he was also hungry.

"That is the trouble with winter,"
said Rabbit, as he hopped outside.
"The colder it is, the more food
I want." He looked around. "And
the colder it is, the less food I find."

There was no green grass.
There was no pink clover.

Rabbit had to make do with brown.

Brown leaves.

Brown bark.

A brown acorn.

When Rabbit saw the words on the tree,
he dropped the acorn in surprise.

The acorn rolled.
It gathered snow.
It turned into a small snowball.

Rabbit read the message.

"Oh dear," he said. "A little bit of *what?*"

The wind blew, icy cold. Rabbit looked down at the snowball, and remembered.

"A little bit of *winter*," he said.

Rabbit rolled the snowball
over the snow.

It grew bigger and bigger.

Rabbit wrapped the snowball
in leaves. "They will keep the
warm out. They will keep the
cold in," said Rabbit.

"Then I shall store it
underground."

Spring came. The sun shone. The snow melted
and the lake turned back to water.
Hedgehog woke up.

"Hedgehog!" said Rabbit.
"Rabbit!" said Hedgehog.

"Oh, Rabbit," said Hedgehog,
"you have eaten *winter*."
"No," said Rabbit. "I ate the bark.
Winter I have saved. It is in my
burrow. I shall fetch it for you."

Hedgehog poked at the soft,
brown ball.
"You told me that winter
was hard and white," he said.
"And cold."
"Just wait," said Rabbit.

He pulled off the leaves,
one by one.

Hedgehog stared at the snowball.
It looked like winter.

Hedgehog sniffed the snowball.
It smelled like winter.

Hedgehog grasped the snowball in his paws.

"*Ouch*," he cried. "It *bit* me."

"*That*," said Rabbit, "is what winter feels like."

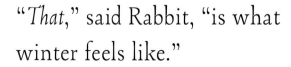

"Thank you for remembering," said Hedgehog.
"I remembered because I missed you,"
said Rabbit. "Did you miss me?"

Hedgehog sighed. "Oh, *Rabbit*," he said.